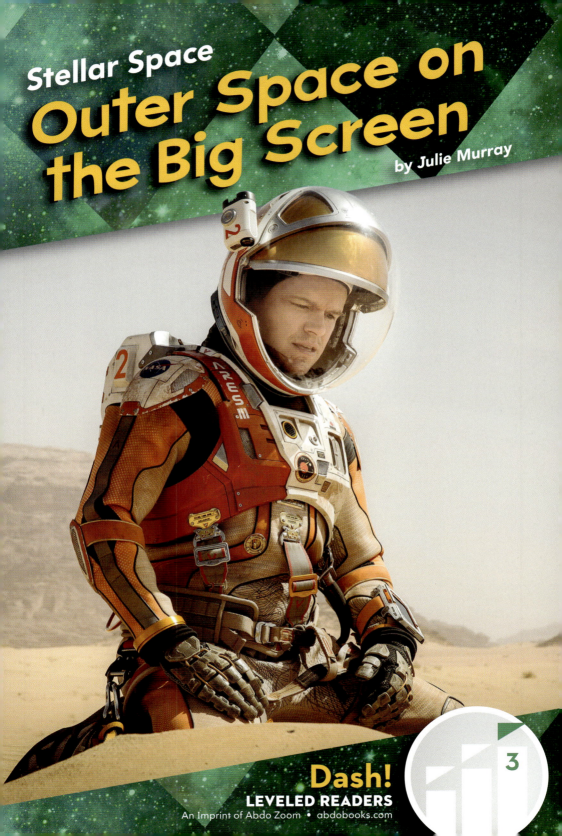

Stellar Space
Outer Space on the Big Screen

by Julie Murray

Dash!
LEVELED READERS
An Imprint of Abdo Zoom • abdobooks.com

3

Level 1 — Beginning
Short and simple sentences with familiar words or patterns for children who are beginning to understand how letters and sounds go together.

Level 2 — Emerging
Longer words and sentences with more complex language patterns for readers who are practicing common words and letter sounds.

Level 3 — Transitional
More developed language and vocabulary for readers who are becoming more independent.

abdobooks.com

Published by Abdo Zoom, a division of ABDO, PO Box 398166, Minneapolis, Minnesota 55439. Copyright © 2022 by Abdo Consulting Group, Inc. International copyrights reserved in all countries. No part of this book may be reproduced in any form without written permission from the publisher. Dash!™ is a trademark and logo of Abdo Zoom.

Printed in the United States of America, North Mankato, Minnesota.
052021
092021

Photo Credits: Alamy, Everett Collection, iStock, Shutterstock
Production Contributors: Kenny Abdo, Jennie Forsberg, Grace Hansen, John Hansen
Design Contributors: Candice Keimig, Neil Klinepier, Victoria Bates

Library of Congress Control Number: 2020919713

Publisher's Cataloging in Publication Data

Names: Murray, Julie, author.
Title: Outer space on the big screen / by Julie Murray
Description: Minneapolis, Minnesota : Abdo Zoom, 2022 | Series: Stellar space | Includes online resources and index.
Identifiers: ISBN 9781098226275 (lib. bdg.) | ISBN 9781098226411 (ebook) | ISBN 9781098226480 (Read-to-Me ebook)
Subjects: LCSH: Outer space--Juvenile literature. | Outer space--Exploration--Juvenile literature. | Outer space in motion pictures--Juvenile literature. | Motion picture industry--Juvenile literature. | Astronautics--Juvenile literature.
Classification: DDC 791.43615--dc23

Table of Contents

Early Films 4

Based on Real Events 8

Space in the Future 16

Space Documentaries 22

Glossary 23

Index 24

Online Resources 24

Early Films

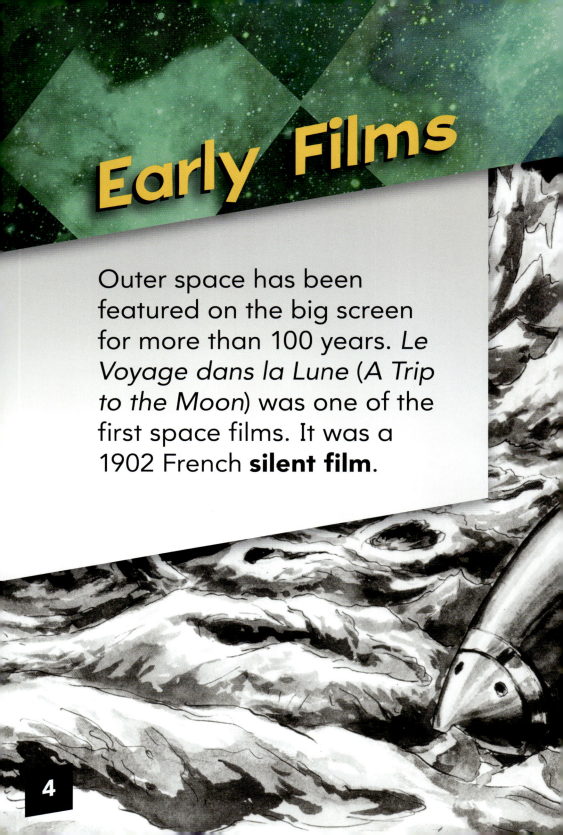

Outer space has been featured on the big screen for more than 100 years. *Le Voyage dans la Lune* (*A Trip to the Moon*) was one of the first space films. It was a 1902 French **silent film**.

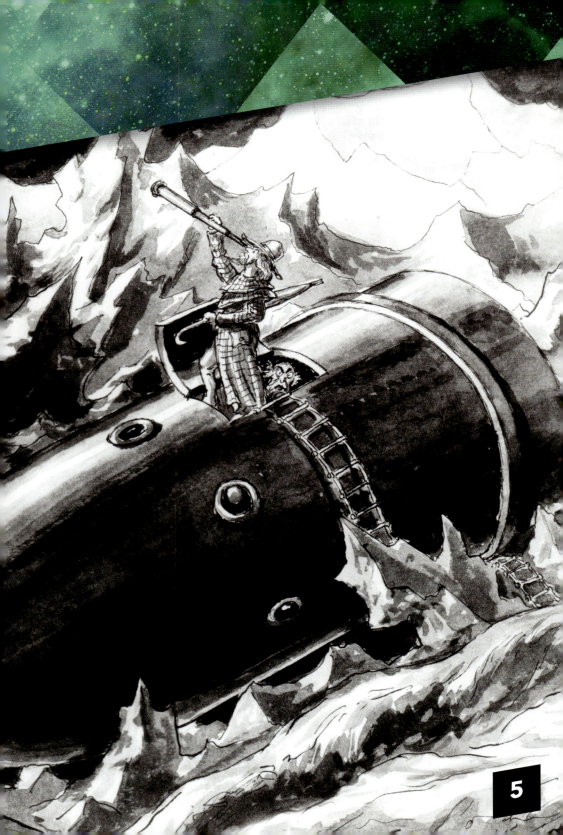

In 1968, *2001: A Space Odyssey* was released. It won an **Oscar** for Best Visual Effects. It is a **science-fiction** movie. It takes viewers on a space adventure. It is known for **accurately** showing space flight.

Based on Real Events

Many space movies are based on real events. *The Right Stuff* (1983) is about the first 15 years of the US space program. It focuses on the lives of the Project Mercury astronauts. This was the first human spaceflight program in the US.

Tom Hanks starred in *Apollo 13* (1995). The movie is about the rescue and recovery of Apollo 13. The spacecraft was damaged in an explosion during flight. The crew's journey back to Earth was heroic in many ways!

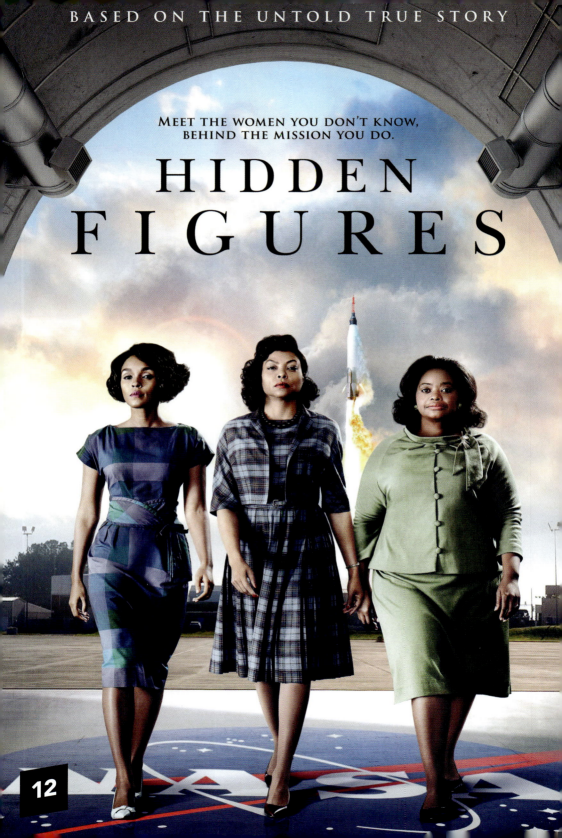

Hidden Figures (2016) is about three Black, female **mathematicians** who worked at NASA. They played an important role in NASA's early missions. Without them, the US Space Program would not have been as successful or as safe.

Ryan Gosling stars in *First Man* (2018). It is about the life of Neil Armstrong. On July 20, 1969, Armstrong became the first person to walk on the moon. The film shows his life leading up to that historic moment.

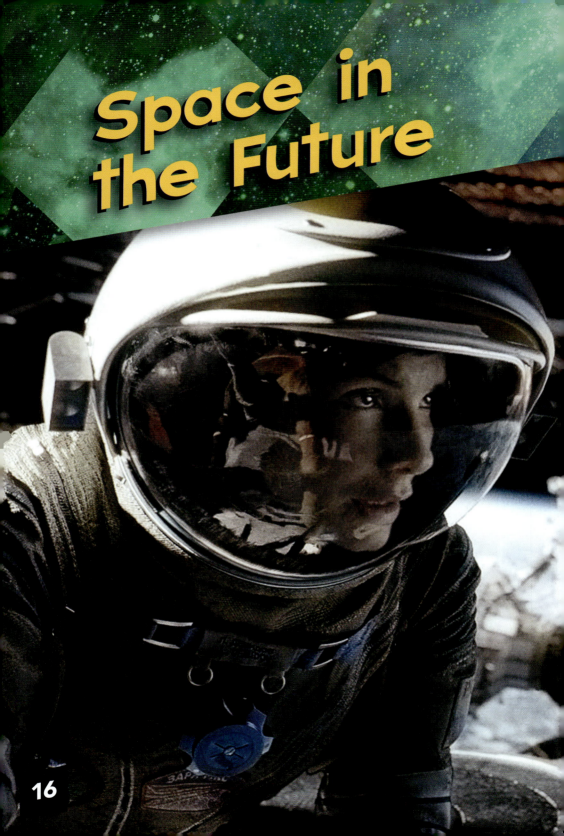
Space in the Future

Some space films are about things that could possibly happen. Sandra Bullock stars in *Gravity* (2013). It is about astronauts stuck in space. They try to find safety as they make their way back to Earth. The film won seven **Oscars**.

Matt Damon plays the **lead role** in *The Martian* (2015). It is about an astronaut who is left behind on Mars. It shows how he survives on the planet and his journey home.

Movies about space are exciting. They give us a preview of what it is like to be above the Earth. Movies also help us think about what space travel could lead to next!

Space Documentaries

- ***In the Shadow of the Moon*** (2007) - about the United States' crewed missions to the moon

- ***Hubble*** (2010) - about Space Shuttle missions to repair and upgrade the Hubble Space Telescope

- ***The Last Man on the Moon*** (2014) - a close look at Apollo astronaut Gene Cernan and his mission to the moon

- ***Journey to Space*** (2015) - unveils a new era of deep-space exploration

- ***Mission Control: The Unsung Heroes of Apollo*** (2017) - about the special team in Mission Control who helped put man on the moon

- ***Apollo 11*** (2019) - focuses on the 1969 mission and includes never-before-seen footage

Glossary

accurately – correctly; without making any mistakes.

leading role – the most important character role in a film or play.

mathematician – an expert in mathematics.

Oscar – the statue given by the Academy of Motion Picture Arts and Sciences in recognition of an Academy Award.

science-fiction – of or pertaining to fiction in which scientific findings, capabilities, or speculations provide an essential basis for the imagined events.

silent film – a film without any sound, especially without spoken dialogue.

Index

2001: A Space Odyssey 6

Apollo 13 11

Armstrong, Neil 14

awards 6, 17

Bullock, Sandra 17

Damon, Matt 18

First Man 14

Gosling, Ryan 14

Gravity 17

Hanks, Tom 11

Hidden Figures 13

Le Voyage dans la Lune 4

Martian, The 18

NASA 13

Project Mercury 8

Right Stuff, The 8

United States Space Program 8

Online Resources

To learn more about outer space on the big screen, please visit **abdobooklinks.com** or scan this QR code. These links are routinely monitored and updated to provide the most current information available.